FARTING SLOTH
COLORING BOOK

SOME SHORT WORDS

The Coloring does exist since many, many year! We know from Colorings since since the antiquity! Even the Mayas used Colorings. Today are Colorings more popular than ever! People use it to reduce stress or just for relaxation.

This Coloring Book for Adults was created with much love. I hope you like the many different pictures. But before you beginn, you can test your color on the right page and see how your colors look on the paper.

Every picture is on the right side. That prevents that the color pushes trough. Furthermore, there are a lot of people that want to cut out their picture and hang it onto the wall.

But now, i wish you a lot of fun with this Coloring Book!

P.S.: If you like the book, i would be very happy if you leave a review on Amazon.com! It takes just a few sconds and would help me a lot! :)

All the best,

Amy A.

TEST YOUR COLORS

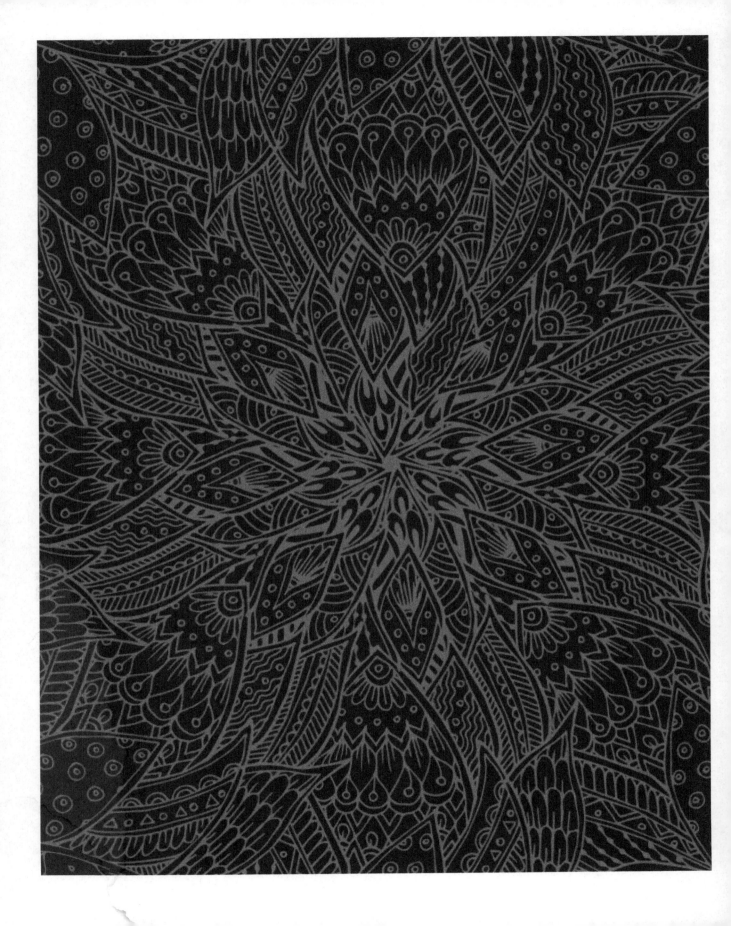

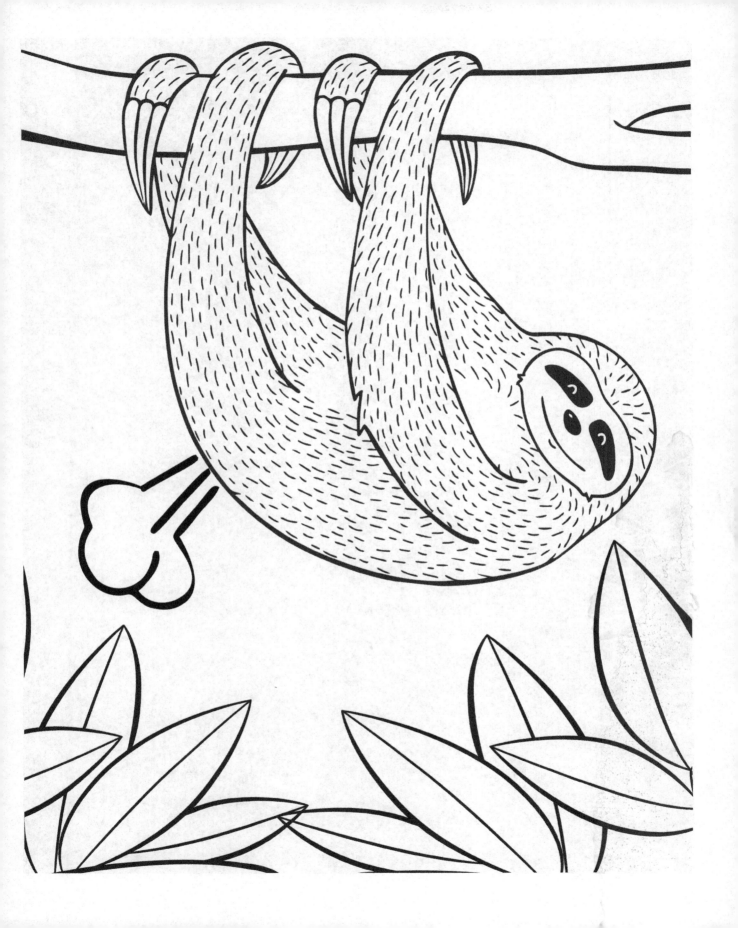

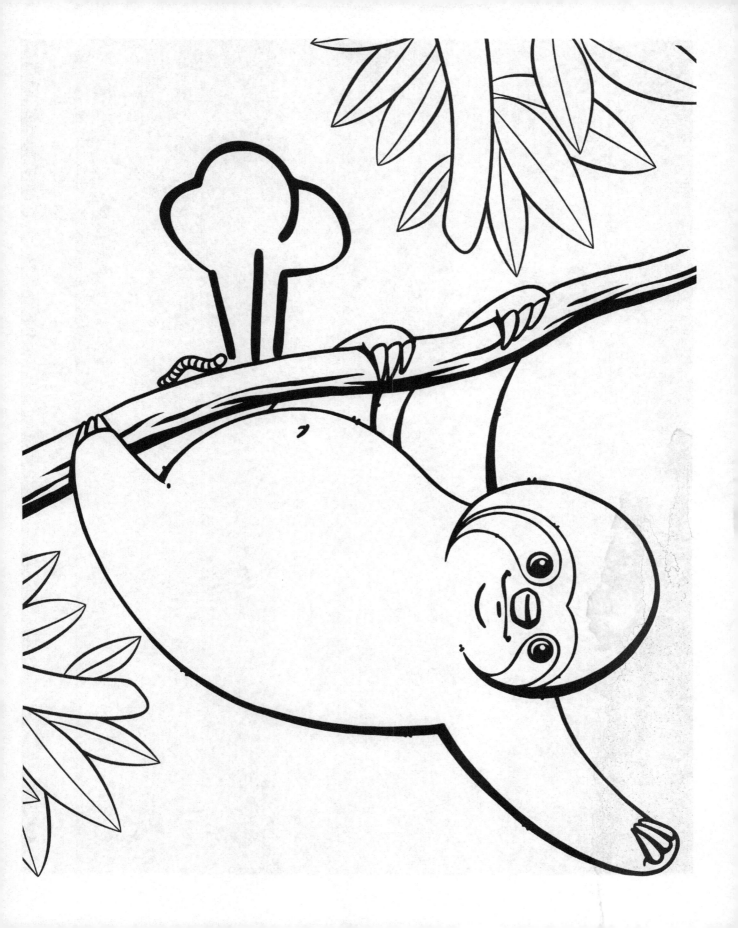

Made in the USA
Coppell, TX
01 February 2020